JPIC Chi Bagule
Baguley, Elizabeth
Yao yuan de jia = A long way
from
home /

34028072754964
FM   ocn258767797
10/08/09

3 4028 07275 4964
HARRIS COUNTY PUBLIC LIBRARY

S0-ACS-091

DISCARDS

A Long Way from Home
遥远的家

〔英〕伊丽莎白·拜格雷 文
〔英〕珍·查普曼 图
思 铭 译

This book belongs to:
这本图画书属于：_____

At bedtime in the burrow, Moz was squished and squashed by sleepy rabbits.

"Oh no!" he tutted. "Crumplings! Move over, Tam."

夜晚的地洞里，小兔子莫莫快被其他的兔子给挤扁了。

"哎呀，别挤啦！"他生气地说。"挤得我皱皱巴巴的！往那边去点儿，塔塔。"

Tam squeezed over then folded her arms round Moz, using him as a hot water bottle.

"Too hot!" muttered Moz.

"Too many rabbits!"

So out into the night he went.

塔塔往边上挤了挤，然后，她把小胳膊搭在莫莫身上，把他当成暖水袋了。

"太热了！"莫莫小声地抱怨说。"这里兔子太多了！"

于是他逃到外面去了。

"What are you doing out here, Smallest Bun?" asked Albatross, swooping down.

"There's no room," snuffled Moz. "And Tam is always squashing me."

"But she's your favourite sister!"

"It doesn't stop her squashing me," said Moz.

"你在这里做什么呢，小不点儿？"信天翁猛地冲下来问他。

"家里没有地方呆了，"莫莫抽抽鼻子。"塔塔还总是挤我。"

"可她是你最喜欢的姐姐啊！"

"那并不能让她不挤我啊！"莫莫回答说。

So, to cheer him up, Albatross told Moz about the land of the North Star, where there was sky space and snow space.

"No rabbits there!"sighed Moz. "I wish I could come with you to the frozen North."

"Hop on, then, Smallest Bun," Albatross said.

于是，为了让莫莫振作起来，信天翁告诉他有一个叫做北方之星的地方，那里有广阔无垠的天空和一望无际的雪原。

"那里没有兔子！"莫莫叹气说。"我真希望我能跟你一起去那寒冷的北方啊！"

"那你就快跳上来吧，小不点儿。"信天翁说。

Moz squeaked as Albatross lifted into the air.

Under the moon and over the wind she flew. As she soared high, high, higher, Moz held out his paws like wings.

"I'm flying!" he cried.

"Hold tight! It's the North Star!" Albatross shouted.

信天翁带着莫莫冲上天空的时候他高兴得尖叫起来。

在月光里，寒风中，信天翁飞翔着。她骤然升起，越飞越高，越飞越高，莫莫随着她张开双手像翅膀一样伸展着。

"我在飞翔！"他大叫起来。

"抓紧我！这里就是北方之星！"信天翁大喊。

From the North Star came a wild tornado of snow and before Moz could take hold of Albatross, he had toppled into the storm. Swept on the wind he tumbled and rolled ...

从北方之星刮来了一股猛烈的说不清是龙卷风、雪旋风还是龙卷雪的东西，还没等莫莫抓住信天翁，就一头跌进暴风雪中去了。莫莫被卷进风中，跌跌撞撞，滚来滚去……

down ...

往下落啊……

And down ...

落啊……

To land *puff!* in a snowdrift.

"噗通！"一声掉进一个大雪堆里，溅起一片雪花！

Moz was all alone and for a moment he was afraid.
Then he looked around at the empty white space
and shook himself with excitement.
"No squish!" he cried. "No squash!"

这里除了莫莫空无一人，一时间他觉得很害怕。后来，他望见四周洁
白的广阔空间，终于不再害怕，而是兴奋起来了。
"不挤啦！"他大叫。"再也不挤啦！"

Moz danced solo in the snow. He skated and skimmed and threw snowballs, but then *whoosh!* he was slipping down an ice slide, going faster and faster.

莫莫一个人在雪地里跳舞。他一会儿滑冰，一会儿滑雪，一会儿又扔雪球。然而，"嗖"地一声，他滑到一片冰上，沿着冰路越滑越快。

Moz skidded to a stop. Oh no!
There were rabbits everywhere!
As he opened his mouth to protest, the other rabbits
did too- but the only sound was Moz's tiny squeak.

莫莫努力地滑雪想要停下来。噢天哪，不！

这里到处都是兔子！

正当他要开口抗议，其他的兔子也跟他一样这么做啦?———但是除
了莫莫小声的尖叫，却没有其他兔子的声音。

"Mirror rabbits!" he gasped.
    There were no other rabbits, just
reflections in the ice.

"镜子里的兔子！"他猛地吸了一口气。
那里并没有其他的兔子，只不过是冰中的照影罢了。

Moz was in an ice cave, an ice hall, an ice palace!
It was as big as space and as quiet as silence.
And there was no one there but him.

原来莫莫跌到了一个冰雪的洞穴里面，冰雪大厅，冰雪
宫殿！寂静的宫殿里只有莫莫自己！

In the mirror-walls Moz saw himself like a king, his fluff grand with ice crystals.

　　在"镜子"墙上，莫莫看见他自己就像个国王一样，冰雪的结晶让他的绒毛看起来庄严美丽。

Moz made a cool, roomy snow-nest.
"No nest- sharings!" he pronounced and
lay royally down to sleep.

莫莫用雪花做了一个凉快又宽敞的安乐窝。

"不用再跟大家挤一个窝啦！"他大声宣布着，像国王一
样地趴下睡觉。

When Moz woke, his fluff was frozen and he was cold to the bone. He lay all alone, shivering, thinking about his snugly sister Tam, squeezed into the nest with all the cosy night-snufflings of his family. Even his tears froze. How he longed to go home!

当莫莫醒来的时候，他的绒毛已经结冰了，他感觉到刺骨的寒冷。

莫莫一个人孤孤单单地躺着，冻得哆哆嗦嗦，心里想着他暖暖的姐姐塔塔，还有一家人挤在窝里温暖舒适的……。就连他流下的眼泪都结冰了。他是多么渴望回到家里去啊！

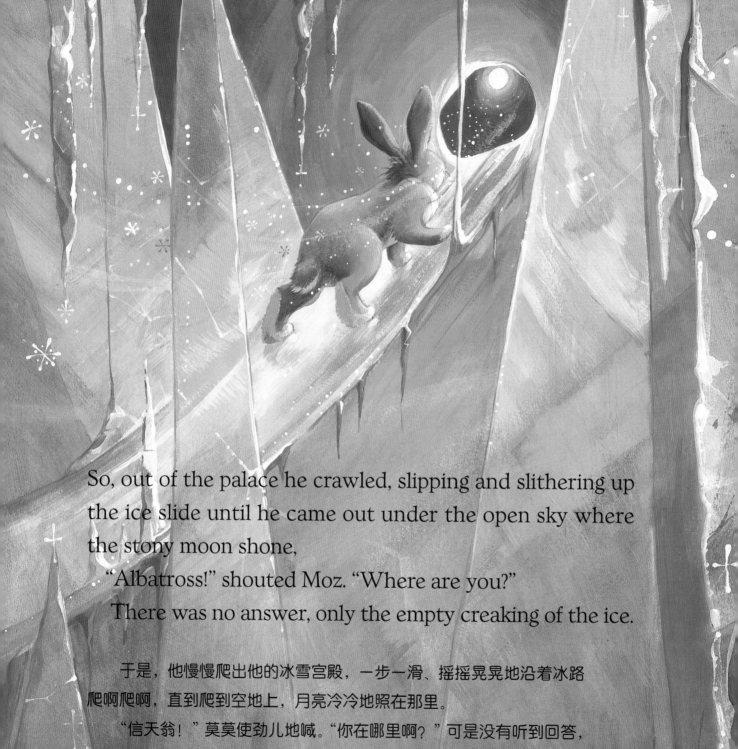

So, out of the palace he crawled, slipping and slithering up the ice slide until he came out under the open sky where the stony moon shone.

"Albatross!" shouted Moz. "Where are you?"

There was no answer, only the empty creaking of the ice.

于是，他慢慢爬出他的冰雪宫殿，一步一滑、摇摇晃晃地沿着冰路爬啊爬啊，直到爬到空地上，月亮冷冷地照在那里。

"信天翁！"莫莫使劲儿地喊。"你在哪里啊？"可是没有听到回答，只有冰块嘎吱嘎吱的碎裂声空空荡荡地响着。

But there! A feathery whisper on the wind. Moz looked up and saw wide wings. It was Albatross!

"Smallest Bun!" she said, relieved. "I've been looking for you everywhere!"

可是，突然！风中传来了像羽毛一样轻柔的声音。莫莫抬起头，看见了伸展开的宽阔翅膀。那是信天翁！

"小不点儿！"说着，她终于放心了。"我一直在到处找你！"

She swung Moz on to her back and gratefully he nestled into her warm down, thinking only of home.

信天翁把莫莫放到自己的背上，莫莫感激地依偎在她温暖的绒毛里，心里只想着他的家。

Back in the nest, Tam rolled over.
Moz was wonderfully squished and squashed; he was
gorgeously crumpled and crammed.
He was Tam's hot water bottle. He snuggled into her
fluff and, with a sigh, he fell to sleep.

回到窝里，塔塔正翻了个身。
莫莫开心地被挤得扁扁的，愉快地被压得皱皱巴巴。
他是塔塔的暖水袋。
他依偎在塔塔的绒毛里，舒了一口气，进入了梦乡。